THE SAINT.

†

The Phantom Origins, A Phantom Queen Companion.

1.

For my mom who started my love of books while I was in the womb, and to my dad, who always did the voices.

Chapter One.

Near the coast of Spain, Spring 1700.

Piranesi watches the silhouette of his wife and son disappear into the moonlit horizon.

Her last words to him before they went to bed, he knows, will haunt his dreams for a long time.

"Be careful the nets you cast, Piranesi. The Sea is always watching, and so am I."

He had tried to brush it off immediately after. But Danae was…a special kind of sea creature. Not human like the rest of them. He had rubbed his temples as he watched her in secret from the Crow's Nest. Normally he didn't stir when she moved in bed, but something was different about the cold spot she had left beside him that night. It felt final. She had gathered their son from his hammock near the bed and carried him to a lifeboat while he scurried up the main mast to watch her. Both he and Danae had ordered the lookout to keep silent, he knew, but when Piranesi ordered it, he received a seething glare that preceded the obedience.

The rising tide of rebellion had been but a faint taste in the air for a while, but recently, as his son grew older, and kinder, and Piranesi stayed the same; his faithful crew had begun to grow sharklike teeth. He rubs his jaw. *It's a problem her absence should remedy.*

He returns his gaze to the dancing sea, cradling the boat that holds his former life as they row away. He breathes a sigh of relief. *Who knew lifeboats don't just save those inside of them? I feel better already.* He peeks up from the water. The last tendrils of his wife's hair fade into the horizon. A giddy laugh bubbles up from his chest and finally, he sinks into the symphony of his true love's secret song. Danae had been suppressing her call for a long time. Now, with her magic no longer suffocating him and the whole crew to 'keep the peace,' he can finally breathe. He takes an extra deep breath, reveling in the feeling of the full expansion of his lungs. The further Danae rows, the louder his curse's call becomes.

He flips onto his back and faces the stars, he can almost taste the victory of finally finding her, Andromeda's Daughter. The other half of a wager the old gods made so long ago. He kicks his feet up, recalling his father's words as though he is speaking them now.

It passes on, from father to son, and mother to daughter. Over and over and over. We must find her, the descendant of Andromeda, every son of Perseus is given the same mission and plagued with the same visions. If we don't find her before the curse passes on to the next son, it drives us mad.

Piranesi shifts uncomfortably, from either the memory or the hard wood planks, he's uncertain. *It's no use to dwell on that now, she's gone, and I can hear the calling that much clearer.* He takes a moment to refocus his breathing, and sink into the memory of his last vision, faint as it was. *What did she look like again?*

He closes his eyes against the twinkling starlight and allows himself to fully feel the moment and watch her in his mind's eye. *Her long hair* he recalls, *it cascades in waves down her back, as dark and alluring as the sea.* He brushes his dark curly hair from his eyes.
So many times, he's seen her form sway like the water, and rip him from his feet like the undertow. He bites his cheek. *What would it be like to finally feel her skin?*

She is as forbidden as the land he cannot touch.

He contemplates, as he had thousands of times before: *what would be more thrilling? Will it be touching land without the fear of death, or feeling her olive skin against mine?* The echo of her laughter calls like a Siren from the depths of his falsest memories. He had seen her so many times in visions. *It's almost better than reality.* He licks his lips and plucks at a whisker, frustrated that her face is the only thing he can never see.

Are her lips red like the roses I've seen from afar, or are they brown and taste as sweet as London chocolate?

He taps his chin, releasing the hair. *Are her eyes blue like the sea, or are they as gold and watchful as the sunset horizon?*

He rubs his eyes with his calloused hands. *Fantasizing about her will do nothing but make the visions intense, he chastises himself.* He spares a glance upward to gauge the stars. It must be past midnight now.

Quietly, he makes his way down from the Nest to the deck, feeling suspicious eyes on his back all the way down. His feet thump with the landing.

The lookout's voice comes out in a low tone at his back.

"You won't last a week without her."

Heat pricks at the back of his neck and anger colors his voice. Who is this no name that challenges him? "She left you, I didn't. Your loyalty lies with me."

"Our loyalty," the lookout shrugs, "is in that lifeboat."

Piranesi loops his thumbs on the waistband of his trousers, digging around in his mind for a name to address the lookout by, scraping for a rank to drop him to. But this boy, like the others, all blend in together, each becoming as faceless as the last. "We'll see about that," he smiles back, "once I tell the rest of the crew she abandoned them, and took her *favorite* son with her."

Piranesi turns to go, when another biting comment stops him in his tracks.

"You don't think she thought of that?" The lookout leans on the main mast and picks his nails.

"She's protected us for years, you think because she's gone, that stops?"

He can't help but take the bait. "What do you mean?"

The lookout pushes himself off the mast and approaches, responding in a low voice.
"Do you really think, after all the years she spent keeping the peace, making sure your…temper, was well placated, she didn't design a way of telling us whether or not you did her in?"

Piranesi almost laughs. "So what? You're telling me she gave you all a code word?"

The lookout cocks his head to the side, and shrugs. "I know it, and you have nothing. Who do you think the crew will believe? A man whose wife abandoned him in the dead of night after years of violent tantrums, or one of their own?"

A wash of stone-cold fear makes its way from his head to his toes. *He has to be bluffing. A code word? Truly, it's ridiculous. He scowls at the man. But is it? A secret song is how all Saint's start their*

three tests. It isn't out of realm.
"How much for your silence?"

A smile stretches across his face. "A month's wages. Upfront. That'll buy, oh I don't know…a fortnight?"

Piranesi bites his tongue. *What's to stop me from disposing of him right now?*
Danae's words break through the thought. *The Sea is always watching, and so am I.* How many times had she warned him that the water keeps score, had warned him of the consequences of taking a life at sea? He taps his fingers on his legs. "Wait here."

He unlocks the treasure hold and tosses a small bag of silver at the lookout, the tinkling of coins cracks through the silence and makes his hair stand on end.

The lookout catches it easily. He opens the pouch and takes a moment to count the contents. He smirks up at him. "Pleasure doing business with you, Captain. I expect another payment in a fortnight."
He slinks back into the shadows, with only the sound of silver alerting the silence to his presence.

Piranesi gulps and makes his way to his quarters. Something about the exchange feels final, dangerous. He shuts the door with an imperceivable snick behind him. He removes his clothing and stares at the empty bed, at the twisted sheets where his wife used to lay. What should have been a sweet relief, sours at the back of his throat. *Danae had been tamping down all of their temperaments, not just mine. His hands begin to tremble, and he grasps them together to stop the shake. What have I just traded?*

He makes the bed and smooths the sheets, trying to distract himself from all the warnings he had been given. All of Danae's ramblings about balance and equal trade comes rushing back. He had driven her away and received the full force of his visions back, but it's almost no use if the crew turns on him first. He lays down on the center of the bed and stretches out in all directions.

He reaches for the spot Danae used to lay and hovers his hand just above the sheets. If he concentrates, he can just feel some leftover energy she left behind. The calming effect of whatever power she possesses, calms his nerves just enough that his hands stop shaking. His heartbeat slows, and finally, he drifts off to sleep.

✝

Piranesi awakens to a beam of morning sun shining through a porthole onto his eyelids He wipes the sleep from his eyes and for a moment, tranquility occupies every cell of his body. But the moment passes, and the threats from the lookout the night before come rushing back.

What am I going to tell the crew?

He crosses the room and uses the bucket in the corner to wash his face, hoping the cold water will inspire a stroke of brilliance. But it does not. He squares his shoulders and opens the door, coming face to face with his first mate; and bumps his forehead into Carlos's chest.

He takes a step back, lowering his arm from the start of a knock. "Oh, sorry about that Captain."

Piranesi rolls his shoulders. "Don't dwell on it."

Carlos furrows his brow and follows him towards the helm. "You look bright this morning," he offers.

Piranesi barely meets his eye, far too distracted with plotting to appropriately respond. "Yes, it's a, a beautiful day, to chase the coattails of fate."

Carlos swivels on his heel and cocks his head to the side. Over fifteen years of service and friendship had made his senses sharp to his Captain's every mood.
"What makes today different than all the last?"

Piranesi ignores the hovering presence of his first mate. *I need to focus before he realizes something is wrong.*
"Just a feeling." His eyes flit side to side. The visions Andromeda's Daughter is starting already this morning. She somersaults down the main mast rope and ends with her nose inches from the deck in his periphery.

Carlos shrugs, feigning nonchalance. "Okay, well we're near Spain. We should port and sell the cargo we have, get our men paid and ship out for more bounty."

Piranesi bristles at his first mate's use of the word, 'our.' The lookout's comment replays in his mind; would Carlos turn on him too if the crew began a mutiny?
"No."

Carlos raises a brow. "No? But Captain, we're nearly a month behind schedule. The Crown is expecting us to deliver shipment or at least report back. If we don't pay the men, they'll leave at the next place we port."

That's exactly why I don't want to port in Spain right now.
He rubs his forehead, turning over how to respond before opening his mouth.
Danae was originally from Barcelona. Her accent and insistence of teaching Vóreios Catalan before Spanish makes that obvious enough.
He chews on his cheek and ignores Carlos's impatient foot tapping.
If we port in Spain and Danae doesn't make an

appearance, the crew will abandon ship anyway to look for her.

"We won't meet the Crown's quota anyway with what little we have. Remember there were at last two of them I wanted to indenture myself."

"But—"

"I said no!"

Piranesi's patience had already worn thin, far quicker than normal. *God, how much had Danae been taming me?* The lone aria of Andromeda's Daughter that replies is answer enough.

Carlos takes a step back, now on high alert. "Where's Danae?" he glances back at the Captain's Quarters. "And Vóreios?"

The question stirs a dangerous whirlpool in the base of Piranesi's stomach. His mind spins on the edge of a pit of self-preservation. *Am I really that different?*

"They're not our concern anymore."

Carlos grabs his arm and leans in. "Did you do something to them?" He hisses.

Piranesi yanks his arm away, quite offended. He guffaws. "You know Davy Jones does not tolerate murder on the Seas!" He shakes off the memory of Carlos's touch.

"Especially when it's one of his…creatures. Inhuman as she was."

The venom in his voice surprises even himself.

"Was?" Carlos immediately catches on. "What do you mean, 'was'?"

He levels his first mate with a raging glare, his temper now about as thin as ice over a boiling pot. *I need to keep this more under wraps before everything topples over.*

The first mate raises his hands in surrender, suddenly changing his tune.

"Okay, I'm sorry. I believe you."

Piranesi's whirlpool calms to a ripple. *That was quicker than he normally backs off…* The pleasant song of his lost lover's voice teases his ears, pulling him from the thought. He shakes himself to focus.

"We need to head south. We'll tell the men they're ill and do not wish to be seen."

Carlos stares at him in confusion. "South? What on earth are you planning to find in the South?"

Andromeda's Daughter prances along the ship's siderail in an impressive balancing act.
I have to, at least, tell him and get someone on my side, or else no one will be.
He shifts his eyes to the right. "She's back."

Carlos turns the wheel per his Captain's command. He raises his eyebrows.
"As in, the curse is active again? I thought Danae took care of that."

Piranesi tamps down the irritation at Carlos's mention of Danae *taking care* of anything involving him.
"Yes, her and I, reached an agreement."

The morning bell breaks up their conversation.

"Fresh slop!" The head cook laughs as he piles steaming mush onto Piranesi's plate.

He forces a laugh, though his mind wanders to the morning's conversation. He joins his first mate at a table and digs in absentmindedly. He scans the tables that his crew sits at, all in clusters. Why had he never noticed that they all form in groups, hunched over and whispering amongst themselves? What could they possibly be discussing?
How long until the lookout spills his secret? Once more he fishes around his mind, trying to remember his name, but nothing comes to him.
I really need to be more involved when Carlos decides to hire.

The second and third mate walk side by side towards them and puts Piranesi at ease. *At least they aren't avoiding me.*
Henrique and Moses, respectively, join on the opposite side of the table. Close as brothers, and visually as similar, with matching mops of blonde hair and wide hazel eyes, you would never see one without the other.

The third mate jostles the table with his knee as he sits down.

"Where's the wife and boy?" Henrique asks with a full mouth.

The second mate, Moses, gives him a dirty look. "Callarte, Gordo!"
He elbows Henrique's side. "Hasn't your mother taught you manners!"

He furrows his brow before staring back. "She's dead actually."

Piranesi fights rolling his eyes, though he's grateful for the normalcy. *At least this morning's ritual is the same.* The immature predictability, though irritating, can only be expected from a crew made up of mostly, orphaned or impoverished teenaged boys. But he supposes, dead parent jokes are a fair exchange for cheap labor.

"Really though," Moses stuffs his mouth and picks up where Henrique left off, "where's the kid? He's normally at my side like a dog."

He forces a smile and tries to tame his jumping heart. "Him and the wife have both taken ill." He clears his throat. "He'll be back to…yapping at your heels, soon."

"Captain!" A cabin boy bursts into the dining hall. "Captain!"

Piranesi's heart lodges in his throat and makes it impossible to breathe. *This is it. I'm done for.* He quickly composes himself. *Pull yourself together and think!* "What's the matter, boy!"

The boy nearly trips over himself. His voice cracks as he shouts. "Danae is gone!"

The stone drops fully into the pit of Piranesi's stomach and immediately makes him sick. The room begins to tilt, and his hands go numb.

"Ah she's sick boy, leave her alone!" Moses chastises him.

A small trickle of relief flows through his chest. At least someone believes him. *Just stick to the lie, you'll be fine!*

But the young boy falls to his knees at Piranesi's feet, panting. "No Captain, you don't understand! There's a lifeboat missing!"

Chapter Two.

Piranesi releases the swallowed panic as he slams his chamber door behind him.

Carlos follows close behind.

"It's time to come clean now Captain." He says as he takes in the surroundings of the chambers. Fully noting—as he had suspected—that his Captain's wife and son are indeed gone. He waits a beat before continuing. "You have to tell them she's gone."

But Piranesi is already in the throes of full-blown panic.

"It's too late now," he mumbles, pacing in front of his bed.

How has it unraveled so quickly? He presses his fingers into his temples hard enough to feel pain. *They're going to mutiny, and then we'll both die!*

His mind unravels into a pile of frayed ribbon. The ends knot and loop around a singular thought: *If I die, she dies, and then my chapter closes and my son's begins.*
He pulls at his eyebrows, finding comfort in the small pricks of pain that comes with plucking. Each singular sting brings him back to the moment before spiraling again.

"Captain!"

His first mate's voice brings him fully back to the present. "What?"

Carlos rests his hands on Piranesi's shoulders, as if trying to hold him together.
"Where are they?"

The sentiment of Carlos's gesture battles against the impulse to lie. Heat explodes in his cheeks, and instead, he lets the fear speak. "They'll mutiny."

"What, why!" He forces Piranesi to meet his gaze. "What happened?"

For a moment, Piranesi considers telling the truth, about everything. The fight, the warning, the lookout, all of it.
He'll never believe me. The certainty of it clamps around his heart.
"They're gone! I don't know where they are!"

A soft soprano voice caresses the side of his face and curls around the cage bars of his temper. It teases a sweet release and pulls at the strings of his desire. Her voice continues, and directs his attention inward, to the beating heart of his fear.

You're going to lose them.

Composure returns to his frame and reinforces the iron bars of his self-control. *I will not.* The plan begins to unroll like a map. But the more he tries to read it, the more it tears apart. *I just need to buy more time.*
"They're sick." A chuckle escapes his lips. He locks eyes with Carlos.
"Tell the men that they're here with me. Asleep in

bed, don't you see?"

He gestures at the pristine sheets, his grin widening painfully.

Carlos releases his shoulders and stares back, dumbfounded. "Captain, now is not the time to go dark." He glances around the room, as if to make certain one more time, Danae is not there.

Another laugh escapes his lips in a fracture before they all tumble out in a trail of broken glass. "They're right there Carlos, they're right there." He points again at the empty sheets.

"Don't you see? Go tell the men that you see."

The muscles in Carlos's jaw tighten and his hands fidget. He backs towards the door, sweat beading at his temple. "Alright Captain, alright. I'll go tell them."

The door snicks shut, leaving Piranesi in darkness. He taps his temples nervously with his fingertips and searches for the voice that called him out.

Where are you, where are you?

His mind stretches for an answer. Any answer. But his

mind is split, with no sense of which way to go. Andromeda's Daughter calls to her Son of Perseus, and yet he cannot reply.

The crew. The crew is the bigger issue.

His mind, with outstretched fingers, reaches like a net with indiscriminate webbing. He tries to catch all there is to fathom. From a trophy of a sea creature to the trash other sailors leave behind, the solution swims in an ocean of gnashing teeth.

Be careful the nets you cast, Piranesi. Danae's words break through the chaos.

Anger heats his face. *I'll be damned if I let you control me again.*

Andromeda's Daughter breaks through the darkness, turning his attention entirely away from his wife. She sings to his soul in the ancient way only the other half of his curse can. He tips his head back in the drunken ecstasy the spirit of her presence evokes in him.

He can feel her, his love so faceless and strapped to the rocks; the monster of destiny waiting to swallow her whole.

He squeezes his eyes shut tight. He had forgotten the headaches that came with the visions. Danae had made him forget, had taken away that pain, and yet… *She* should have been his wife, he fumes. *Not* Danae. *She* should have been the mother to Vóreios.

The wind picks up outside and rattles his window.

His mind snaps into focus. *No. No there has to be a way.*
His curse, his untouchable queen of the sea. She is the sole mission, not the bounty or the money, or the thrill of the chase. Her. Whoever she is. *My crew is getting in the way.*

He hits his bedpost with the side of his fist. *I can't man the ship alone.*
The lookout's words make his skin crawl. *I can't just lie, not when she's already planted seeds for the truth.*

He crosses the room and raps his knuckles on his dresser. He casts a slightly more narrow net to the solution, and ticks off a list in his mind: He can't man the ship alone. He needs his men to be by his side, and they need to believe he had nothing to do with it. His mind spins like a whirlpool, encircling a single thought.

Their abandonment isn't enough. They need to have no room for doubt.

He paces the length of his room still scrambling for the perfect answer. The irony of his predicament does not fail to hold his attention captive. He pinches his chin. *I was trapped with them here, and I am trapped with them gone.*

A gaggle of shouts and draws his attention to the other side of the chambers. He cracks his door just slightly and presses an eye to the gap of light.

"Where are they Carlos?" the crew demands.

Carlos shows his palms, a placating gesture of surrender. He keeps his tone of voice low and steady. "I just laid eyes on them in the Captain's quarters. They're both ill, but they will recover."

"Then why haven't I seen them!" The ship's surgeon shoves forward, his medicine bag in hand. "Better yet, why can't I see them now?" He swings the bag in a wild gesture, nearly taking out the men beside him. "That's my job. Let me see his wife and boy!"

The crowd shouts their assent.

Piranesi slams the door shut. *Shit.*

He sinks to the floor, the splinters of the aged wood catch his shirt.
Why didn't I think to pay off the surgeon?
It would have been the perfect alibi.

He presses his fingers to his temples, picturing how he could have orchestrated it. The surgeon would have entered the room with his bag and corroborated his side.
The crew would certainly believe the surgeon and their Captain over some lookout!
But the image is desperate, flimsy, and melting against the heated reality of the surgeon's pious nature.

A new vision replaces the old. The man would enter his chambers with his medicine bag and self-righteous esteem of his God and declare them both gone.

A shudder rakes down his spine. The crew would turn immediately. They would tear him and his ship apart looking for them, or at least their bodies; and when they come up empty-handed, they'd mutiny. Then where would his destiny land?

The answer stares him plain in the face: In the hands of his boy.

The image of his son appears in his mind's eye as clearly as a physical presence in front of him. He spits at the idea. *My boy. Please. A delicate flounder among sharks.*

He recoils at his own reaction. *Vóreios is my son...*

He mentally recites it like a phrase needing studied, and the words hold no definition. He knocks on the wood floor beneath him. *I need a way out.*

The sea of gnashing teeth offers sacrifice at the altar of his sanity for the sake of a brilliant idea. His mind cracks open.

It could work.

Without another moment's hesitation, he stands and opens the door. "Carlos! Get in here!"

Carlos slips away from the crowd and sprints inside his chambers. Piranesi slams the door shut before the crew can follow.

Carlos stands with his hands on his knees, sweat drips from his brow. "Are you going to tell me where they are?" He pants.

Piranesi scowls back. *Never on your life.* He lifts his chin.
"The crew needs to see them gone, and my hands need to be clean of it."

"Fat chance of that." He stands back upright. "They're ready to mutiny right now."

Piranesi draws his sword, the thin grip he has on his rising panic snaps.
"Are you going to join them?" He taps the point against his first mate's chin.

Carlos knocks the sword aside and rolls his eyes. "We don't have time for this. You either come clean or think of something else right now."

Piranesi's gaze is drawn across the sea, where he can hear her call. The words come before he can process the meaning.

"The crew needs to know they're dead."

"Captain," Carlos lowers his tone to a timid whisper, "what did you do?"

Disgust clenches his gut, and he rises to his own defense. "I told you, I did nothing!" He sniffs, the idea now half-formed. "Where's the nearest line of trade ships?"

Carlos doesn't hide his bafflement. "What are you on about now! What does that have to do with anything!" He runs his fingers through his hair, puffing out his curls. "We don't even have jurisdiction with them unless there's a slave mutiny, and as the crew stands, they're not going to help you!"

But the plan has already been birthed in his mind. It screams for attention, in the same way a newborn cries for its mother, freshly bloodied and ripped from the womb.

Piranesi taps his chin. "Do we have any bodies?"

Carlos blocks the door. "Excuse me? What in god's name are you doing?"

Piranesi lunges at him, "Answer your Captain! Do we have any bodies in the hold!"

"Captain," his voice returns to a timid whisper. "I'm begging you, tell me what you're doing."

Piranesi scoffs and sidesteps his first mate towards his bed. He stretches out on the sheets and yawns. "Tell the men that you've just laid eyes on my wife and son again. Tell them they're alive and mostly well, but do not want visitors."

Carlos bows his head. "I will, now please, tell me what you're doing."

Piranesi ignores him. "You'll bring me two bodies tonight, one big and one small." His voice rings out in a singsong melody as though joining in on the other half of a duet.
"I don't care where you find them, or if you must make them. You can bribe the night lookout if you

like. But bring them to me, and then I want us along a trade ship route by dawn."

Carlos grips the doorknob to hide the shaking in his hands and asks once more.
"What are you doing."

Piranesi kicks off his boots and waves him away. His eyes are already trained on something no one else can see. He continues the silent song.
"Assuring safety old friend. Just assuring safety."

Chapter Three.

Piranesi stares at his chamber ceiling long
after his first mate leaves.
He had been allowing his mind to warp the lines of
wood plank into swirling shapes and energy in the
hours since Carlos's departure. The plan was still
young back then. Desperately young, and he hasn't
the time for natural growth. His ambition has carried
him this far, and it has yet to fail him. He takes it by
an outstretched hand and holds tight.

"I wrap the bodies, and I throw them over."
His voice harmonizes with the silence, still working
out of the kinks of the plan. The crew needs to know
without a shadow of a doubt that she's gone, forever.

"I wrap the bodies, and I throw them over…"
The lancing pain of realization strikes his brain. He
pounds a fist to his forehead. *No, that's stupid. I can't
wrap them, wrapping could lead to unwrapping and
then it's all over. I warp them. I warp them beyond
recognition.*

"I warp the bodies and throw them over."
Another strike. *But what if I'm seen throwing them
over myself. A bag of pulp is not discreet.*

"I warp the bodies, and they throw them
over." He steers this thought before it bites him. *They
need to think it's a foreign ship committing the crime
of tossing an innocent woman and child overboard. I
can't do it myself. But who would be obedient to me
after this morning? It can't be anyone in the crew.*

"I warp the bodies before they come over."
His mind aches as it stretches for answers.
*If I actually allowed a foreign ship to invade The
Gods Curse, it would be more believable. But who
would be barbaric enough, that I become infallible?
The foreign traders are often French.*
He lets loose a chuckle. *Right, like those soft-handed*

men could pull anything this brutal off. The other tradesmen are...

"I warp the bodies before Company's over." A smile tugs at the corners of Piranesi's mouth. *That's it. The English.*

A pleasant tingling had started in his hands and grows from a subtle sensation to a painful series of blades. He sits up and shakes them out. The room's musty smell brings him back to the moment before he's lost in thought once more.

The plan is perfect, infallible. He smiles to himself. *Even if they deny it all, the language barrier will hide the lies.* He just needs to wait on Carlos. *Once the bodies are in my hands, everything will be under control, I'll be safe.*

Piranesi wipes his sweaty hands on his trousers.
Carlos will have to find bodies, and take them from the hold without causing a scene. The ship lays out like a blueprint in his mind. *He'll have to sneak them up from the hull, across the decks, and into my chambers without being seen.*

A nervous tingle settles in his stomach. *What if the lookout sees him?*
But surely, Carlos knows the lookout posts. He wouldn't be that stupid as to be seen.

A small rap comes at his door, he cracks it open.

"Captain," Moses pants, sweat dripping from his brow.

Surprised, he opens the door just long enough for Moses, Henrique, and the body between them to fall inside.
"What are you doing here!" he hisses at them anxiously.

Henrique looks up, confused. "Carlos said you needed this, said it was for Miss Danae?"

At the mention of her name, he begins to search around the room.

Panic darts out from his chest. "Get out!" He lunges in front of the boys, trying to hide the view of the empty bed, and shoves them from the room.

"But!" Moses protests and tries to look back.

"I said out!" He slams the door shut, breathing a sigh of relief once they're on the other side of the door.

What was Carlos thinking! Involving them was stupid and reckless!

He wrings his hands, *the more people that know about the bodies, the more suspicious they'll be when they're found, they might turn on me anyway.*

He would have to talk to his first mate about his reckless behavior. But for now, a job needs done. He looks over at the half-stiff body on the floor.

A bushy haired man, practically skin and bones, lies stiff and warped on his floor. His mouth hangs half-open, his glassy eyes bore a hole through Piranesi's soul.

A chill runs up his spine. He kicks the head away from him. But too late, he recognizes it, from weeks ago. *He was just a scrap of cargo.* He reassures himself.

The negro had escaped his chains aboard a Casa de Contratacíon slave ship, he recalls. He had nearly successfully mutinied and liberated the lot of them.

How embarrassing that would have been for the Crown.

Satisfaction perches like a bird on his chest and sings a song of triumph.

It was a serious enough victory that the ship's Captain had given him a handsome tip for his silence.

Emboldened by the memory, he kneels at the man's side and binds his arms to his torso. The chill of death seeps like the blood that pools beneath his carcass, into Piranesi's flesh. Creaking cartilage and squeaking musculature provides the perfect percussion to the song he sings to distract his mind.

Another knock pulls him from his task.

Carlos gently nudges the door open with his toe and places a smaller body on the bed.

His silence is a reprimand of its own.

After a moment, he speaks. "I don't know what you think it is we're doing, Captain." He stands alongside Piranesi, who's still binding the body. He swallows. "But it's a bad idea."

Piranesi stares back up at him, the moonlight casts harsh shadows on his first mate's face, giving him an eerie appearance of death. He gulps down the small ray of fear that rises in his throat, and quickly replaces it with anger.

"What made you think involving Moses and Henrique was a good idea?"

Carlos is taken aback. "You didn't think I'd be able to carry all that dead weight on my own!"

He stands and gets in his first mate's face. "This ship is on the verge of mutiny, and you think involving boys was the best course of action!"

"Those boys!" Carlos bites back. "Those boys are loyal to a fault, you made sure of that! They have nothing and nobody outside of this ship! You think they're going to throw you under the keel? You're all they have!"

A small ray of comfort warms Piranesi's chest and is almost immediately swallowed by shame. He had made sure to get the most disadvantaged young boys. Some of them barely of age or under.

"They didn't need to be a part of this."

This makes Carlos concede. He sighs, his shoulders slump. "I wish they didn't have to be." He whispers. "But I framed it as though we were giving a sea burial and they offered to help. It wasn't until we were out of earshot that I told them it was for Danae."

Piranesi raises his eyebrows. "I'm shocked they believed you. What kind of person needs bodies to become well?"

He shakes his head. "The men don't know anything about your curse, or about the creature Danae is. But they know there's something special about her." He meets his Captain's eye again. "They love her, like the mother most of them don't have. They would do anything for her and your son."

Piranesi looks back at the body on the floor, at the slave that would become Danae's mascot. *Her death is going to destroy them.*
He considers, for a moment, coming clean. Telling the crew that Danae returned to Spain and took Vóreios with her.
But where would that leave me? I would have no crew, and there's not enough funds to hire all new. I'll

be stranded, docked on land, helpless to leave, and when I no longer have enough money to stay docked? Memories of violent waves of nausea, headaches, and sea water filling his lungs while he drowns on dry land floods his senses. He shudders. *Andromeda's Daughter first. I find her, and I'll release them.* The bargain feels like a devil's deal, but he shakes hands anyway.

He schools his expression into cool indifference. He needs to be steadfast and levelheaded to get the job done. "Make sure there's a ship to intercept and a commotion worthy of chaos."

He kneels back to the floor and returns to the safe steady focus of his work, ignoring Carlos's sighing behind him. "I hope you know what you're doing, Captain."

The door clicks shut.

He uses his feet to turn the man over and tie him off. His back had become purple with his blood, pooling at the lowest center of gravity. He tightens the rope in one swift movement, the force of it ripples his back like a bag full of seawater.

He swallows the bile that burns his throat. *He was just cargo. Inhuman then, and inhuman now.* He presses his tongue to the inside of his cheek. *It has to be done.*

The Sea is always watching, and so am I.

He bats away the thought like a fly. *I'm not hurting anyone. They're already dead. I'm simply making the most of a poor situation.*
He stands and inspects his work, hands on his hips. *Done. I can pose it later.*

He moves over to the corpse laid out on his bed. A miniscule tug of sympathy pulls at a far corner of his mind. *He's so small. Even compared to Vóreios.*
He leans over him, and the sweet smell of rot, curled around the bitter iron of dying flesh meets his nose. He coughs and exhales out of his mouth, as if to blow the stench away. He recognizes this one too.

It's the boy.
He had been aboard the same ship, Piranesi recalls. He was a vicious little thing, willing to scrap with anyone who got too close to his mother. He had hopes

of building him into a good little indenture.

He carefully moves the arm to its side, revealing skin pocked with small dark dots, and open wounds. He grips his chin to turn his face away and his teeth give beneath the pressure. He swallows the sour taste of bile. *He was a boy.*

He takes a step back and searches his heart and mind. *Is there any other way?*
He turns the lookout's words over in his head. *Did Danae really leave a code word?*
If she didn't, he could lie, say she abandoned them. *But I already told them she was sick. It's too late for that now. I have no other choice.*

He shakes out his shoulders. *I can't think about it like that. He's not a human being anymore. There's nothing inside these bodies.*
In the corner of the room, Andromeda's Daughter stares out the porthole.
These are not people. They're tools. If I don't use them, they'll have been a waste.

He kneels back on the bed. *They'll serve a purpose now.*

He ties the remaining length of rope around the boy's body and binds it into a single log. Not stopping to take a breath before moving on, he grabs the man half flopped on the floor by the shoulders. *I should pose this one now.*

Moving without full awareness of his actions, he pulls a knife from his dresser drawer. It glints against the moonlight, like a spark of hope in eternal night. *Just don't think about it.*
He pulls the bedsheets back and lays the bodies on the mattress. He takes a moment to pause. *I don't want to get anything on my clothes.*

Layer by layer, he peels off clothing, until he stands in nothing but his undergarments.
He double checks that there's a bucket of water to clean up with. Then, he spins the blade in his hand and begins cutting.

Piranesi steps away from the bed and inspects his work one more time. His cold hands stick to the torn pieces of flesh on his bed as he inspects every chunk. Yellow beads of fat cling to his fingers and flatten into a creamlike smear against the sheets.

Crimson soaked and littered with flesh the consistency of oatmeal, he tucks the big carcass into bed the same as his wife used to lay. Then, piece by slopping piece, he takes the body of the child and stuffs it into Vóreios's hammock, taking care not to cut his hands on the bone shards.

He laughs despite himself. *Funny, how we all look the same on the inside.*
He crosses the room, dodging Andromeda's Daughter, and takes his time at the water bucket. Making sure every drop of blood and chunk of flesh are clean of his skin, he changes back into his normal clothes. With extreme care, he brings the blood-filled bucket out of his chambers and dumps it over the side of the ship.

"Do I even want to know what you've done?"

He whips around to see Carlos standing right behind him. The pounding of his heart steadies. "What has been done," he responds carefully, "is for the good of the crew and mission."

"Good of the crew?" He scoffs.

Piranesi glares. "Something on your mind?"

He shakes his head, "I'm just wondering how anything matters at this point."
He rests his elbows on the siderail and faces the helm.
"You lost your wife and son, god knows how, and desecrated bodies to cover up your shame."
He shrugs. "Are you even the kind of man your 'true love' would accept at this point?"

Piranesi allows the words to fully sink in before he responds. The blood-soaked bucket is still in his hand, a token of evidence to what he's done. He throws it into the sea. *Everything I've done is to find her, why wouldn't she?*
"What shame? I have done nothing wrong."

"Nothing wrong!" He runs his fingers through his hair, chuckling coldly.
"You're mad if you think you've done nothing wrong."

The ticking clock of his patience has already begun, the pendulum that had been in the cool controlled part of his brain is now beginning to swing towards a manic rage.

What doesn't he understand about the situation?
Danae and Vóreios are gone, and they took the crew's loyalty with them.

He turns to his first mate, clenching his jaw to keep his temper inside.

Without Carlos I lose the crew, without the crew I can't find Andromeda's Daughter.

Piranesi grabs him by the collar and yanks him down, nose to nose. "Fuck. You. I'm the Captain!"

He shoves him away and paces a few steps away.

"Believe me, the irony isn't lost on me Carlos," Piranesi laughs and gestures wildly.

"I have been at sea my whole life." His voice drops to a cool tone.

"I have never known the smell of earth, the touch of a flower, or felt the steadfast stillness of the ground I stand on."

The flood of emotions spill over like a waterfall. He hadn't spoken the words aloud before and now they won't stop. His voice shakes with every syllable.

"Everything has always moved, has always been unsure, has always been as swift as the sea to change. I have received no mercy from the waters I've lived, the curse I carry, or even the woman I married. Any mercy I have ever been shown has been at my own hands, and I will not apologize for giving unto myself generously."

A sorrowful look passes over Carlos's expression. "But do you think she will love you, if she knows?"

"The curse dictates her love for me, she has no choice and therefore, I have nothing to lose. Nothing, except for her."

Carlos follows Piranesi as he walks away, unable to stop the words as they tumble out. "But Danae loved you, and so did your son; and you sacrificed their love for ambition. Will you not squander her love as well?"

The muscle in his jaw begins to twitch. "My love is my ambition. There is nothing outside of her."

Sensing the argument officially closed, Carlos concedes. "Of course, Captain."

Piranesi returns his gaze to the barely lit horizon. The vision of his love dances before him. He taps his finger on the siderail and hums the rhyme he learned as a boy.

They were bound to the sea, with their memories clean, Andromeda and Perseus, their curse falls on the rest of us.

He mumbles it the same way his father had done, and his father, and his father before him. All down the line, until Danae's lips wrapped around the words to tell his son.

Danae, treacherous Saint of the Sea. You deafen my call, you take my purpose, and now you leave me on a knife's edge while my crew turns on me to run to you.

He gestures with his lips towards north. "I see the trade ships, which one is a Company ship?"

"The Company!" Carlos takes his hands off the helm. "As in, the East India Trading Company?" He runs his hands through his hair. "Why on earth would you want one of them!"

Piranesi spares a glance in the direction of his chambers, then fixes his gaze back to the trade ship line. "Only a monster can do what's been done to my wife. An Englishman fits the bill."

"If all you need is an English ship, then pick an English ship, but not the Company, they travel as a fleet, we'll all die!"

Pianesi narrows his eyes, sick of his first mate's defiance. "You think I'm mad!"

He rubs his fists into his eyes. "I think you're desperate. Let me please just get a straggling ship. Not a Company ship, it can be English if we must, but please, not a Company ship."

The edge in Carlos's voice gives him pause. The crew won't follow his orders if he's not on his side. "Very well old friend."

He exhales and runs a hand down his face. "Thank you. There's a small ship off to the west just a bit. English colors but no Company flags. They look like an easy enough target. Just tell me when to sound the alarm."

He turns The Gods Curse towards the lone ship. Their approach, which at first seems steady, speeds up when the ship turns to face them. With little warning, gunfire cracks off the starboard side.

Piranesi grins. "Alarm sounded."

Chapter Four.

Piranesi's heart pounds in his ears in rhythm
with his responding cannon fire.
He stands on the crossbeam of the mizzenmast,
laughing in nervous pre-emptive victory.

"Hurry men!" He goads from his place above
them. "We can't let them get away!"

The winds pick up, the sails snap, and the
waves crash in a scream against sideboards.
Carlos turns at a sharp angle.
Piranesi's feet almost slide off the crossbeam. He
wraps his arm around the mast to stay aloft.

The figures on the opposing ship scramble to reload their weapons.
A small ship without cannons makes for an easy target.

Piranesi smirks, everything is going according to plan. With a cry, he throws a rope to the other ship's mast. The weight he had placed as an anchor, loops around their crossbeam. The ship lurches and catapults him forward.

He lands with a thump on their deck.

"Die!"

He has just enough time to process the English word before dodging the blow.
The wood splinters prick his skin as he rolls. He regains his feet and swings at the back of the man's head.

A dull pain registers in his hand right before the man lands with a thump on deck.
Another shadow cools his back.
He spins.

"Captain, it's me!" Henrique ducks his swinging fist.

The pounding adrenaline calms in his chest. He raises a sword. "We take the ship!"

A trio of battle cries off to the right makes him jump. He charges. His shoulder drives into the man on the far right.

They tumble to the ground. Piranesi kicks out a leg and trips the second man, leaving only one for Henrique to take down.

From the ground, he spares a glance over his shoulder. A few Englishmen have already boarded his vessel.

"Captain!"
Moses blocks a blade from coming down on his head.

Piranesi scrambles to his feet and draws his sword. With a swing he clears the man's head from his shoulders.

A blade cuts the air near his ear. He feints right and follows through with a strike.

Blood sprays his face.

A bone chilling scream comes from his ship. Excitement electrifies his spine. *They've been found!*

On cue, Carlos's voice comes from the deck. "Captain! They got Danae!"

He abandons the fight and sprints like wind, fast as his feet can carry him. His men follow close behind.

He swings from the ropes and lands with a *thunk* back on his ship.

Carlos waits for him with a bloodstained Englishman at the end of his sword.

Now is my chance, my only chance. If this goes wrong, I'm done for.
"What have you done!" He charges the captive.

"Run!" the Englishman wails from his knees. "The devil's aboard this ship!"
The man's cohorts pass by in a blur. One by one, they abandon their crewmate.

Piranesi stands a foot away from the captive. He's covered in blood as though he had been bathed in it. He can almost believe the man had done what he'd been framed for.

He conjures all the rage in his chest. "Where is my wife!"

"I have done nothing!" The man wails in English, a beg for anyone's belief.

Piranesi fights a smirk. Just as he'd expected. English speaking only. He and Carlos are the only two that speak English, and this poor fool doesn't know Spanish.

He switches languages to ask in the sailor's native tongue. "Where is my wife."

The man's eyes grow wide, hopeful. "I'm innocent!"

Carlos steps in closer and holds a blade against his throat. "He ran out of your quarters sir."

With artificial panic, he runs to his chambers. *Please work.* He spares only a glance over his shoulder to call to his men. "We may not be too late!"

He kicks open the door.
The smell had already begun to set in. He gags. A mixture of iron and rotted meat and something distinctly sweet permeates the air.

"Captain, what is that!" Henrique gags and turns his face, trying to gulp down clean air.

Moses holds his shirt over his nose and says between coughs. "I'll go check on them sir." He steps across the threshold, his chest puffed out in a held breath.

A figure shadows the doorway and before he can warn the boy, another Englishman jumps Moses and hold him to his chest.
With one blade at Moses's neck, and the other towards Piranesi, he belts his innocence.
"I won't die for this!" He screams, covered in blood and chunks of flesh.

"Captain, help!" Moses reaches for him. The Englishmen grips him tighter.

"Moses, stop moving!" Henrique rages. "Let him go!"

The man gestures at the retreating ship and then at his captive.

"Let us free and I'll return the boy."

"Put the blade down." Piranesi coos with his hands in the air. "Let him go, or you won't get out of this alive."

The man meets his eyes, a sudden spark of defiance and understanding changes his stance. "Yo no hice—"

Panic floods Piranesi's senses at the same time understanding clicks into place. *I can't let him speak, it'll ruin everything!*
Piranesi charges. "Run Moses!"
He tackles the man to the ground and rains down his fist to shut him up for good.

A sharp pain lances through his leg. A scream escapes his lips.

Henrique charges running his blade through the man's throat. He leans over Piranesi. "Captain, are you okay?"

He registers Henrique's silhouette eclipsing his line of vision. His features are cut harshly in an ominous shadow.

He grips the back of his leg. A hot sticky fluid pools beneath him.

"Captain?" Carlos appears in the doorway. "Oh my god, get the surgeon!"

The edges of his vision darken as the room begins to spin. The smell of carved up flesh and infection bleeds into his nostrils and clouds his mind.

"You saved my life Captain." Moses's voice comes from somewhere far off in the distance. Further than the ringing in his ears.

He has just enough time to register the clamping pain of a tourniquet before everything goes dark.

Danae's glowing face appears out of the darkness.

Her form like a halo, a heavenly body of forgiveness.

She reaches her hand out to him, her pale skin soft as velvet in his calloused hands.

"It's time to let go. You can come home. I'll welcome you home."

He turns away, his body drops from her warmth into a pool of freezing water.

Her glow in saintly clothes sinks further into the distance as he claws his way through the water.

Drowning. He realizes. He's drowning.

A rage of song and color rips through the darkness in a hurricane and tears the air from his lungs.

Her twilight hair is illuminated by starlight as it floats in the water.

It reaches with seductive fingers towards his throat.

I can't breathe.

His lungs are burning, burning like a pillaged ship.

Burning like the hell he belongs in.

Danae's face breaks through the nightmare.

Her brow is furrowed, and sorrow clouds her sharp emerald eyes.

"I told you, be careful of the nets you cast. The Sea is watching."

She glances over her shoulder as if checking to see if someone is behind her.
"Don't take what you can't pay, I'm watching."

He struggles against the weight of the water and protests her warning.

No. No those bodies were dead! They weren't you! They weren't my son!

He thrashes against the current sucking him further below.

I've done nothing wrong!

The Englishman collapses at his side, the blood from his neck rains past his lips and disperses like mist in the water around him.

Iron coats his tongue.

His own image warped and distorted ripples into view, a mirror in front of him.

Fire lights the sea around him, and his ears are flooded with a cacophony of cries.

He opens his mouth to scream, but no sound comes out.

I did what I had to in order to survive!
He protests to the sea as if it will listen.

I was merciful.

I WAS MERCIFUL!

His men continue to burn around him.

But. I. Was. Ruthless.

Chapter Five.

Near the Coast of Acapulco, Mexico. Six weeks later...

"How long since the last vision?" Carlos asks as he turns the ship to port.

Piranesi massages his stiff leg before responding. "About a week."

"And when you were out of it?"

He reflects to the weeks he spent under the surgeon's care, in and out of consciousness. He was awake only long enough to eat and drink. Between the agonizing pain of the tourniquet, the stitches, the burning, and the saltwater washes, the tortured visions of Andromeda's Daughter, were his only company.

Company I'm relieved to have a break from…

He shakes his head, best not to share that. "No, just a restless sleep, the whole time."

Carlos taps his thumb on one of the spokes. "Has she ever gone silent before?"

Piranesi stands and leans on the cane the ship's carpenter had made for him.

"She has. But never for this long."

The empty space where she used to reside begins to lament. Every time she would disappear, he would have these periods of relief before going back to an insatiable hunger for her presence, like a drunk between drinks. He shakes himself out of it; determined to hold on to the temporary peace while he can.

"You weren't present for the memorial," Carlos remarks. "Don't worry, I took care of everything."

He shifts his eyes to Carlos, afraid to ask the question. "Did anyone suspect?

He shakes his head. "No one suspected a thing. Matter of fact, the men think you're a hero, after what you did for Moses."

"Hm…" He considers asking on the status of the crew, they had to scrape the bodies from the bedsheets and hammock, it couldn't have been easy. The image of the two corpses he had defiled, ripen in his mind and leave their rotten stench on his victory. He had left his men to clean it up. *What does it matter? They would be hurt either way.* He exhales, pushing his guilt into his breath and releases it to the air. He hobbles slowly to the siderail of the ship, and tries to shake the dirty feeling from his skin. He glances down, and focuses on his new cane, it was something to get used to.

"Why are we in Acapulco?" He asks.

Carlos calls for the men to weigh anchor before answering. In response, he takes a ring of keys from his pocket and leads Piranesi to the treasure hold.

The door squeaks open and he gestures inside.

A small bag rests on the back shelf. Piranesi picks it up and gives it a shake. *This is far less than I left in here when I paid off the lookout.* Who's been in here? A small sharp jingle comes from the pouch. "Where did it all go?"

Carlos shakes his head. "The men didn't want to pick up bounty without you, after everything we went through with the English ship, you're their conquering hero. So, we scraped by and traded with a few ships on the way, until we made to port here. Don't worry, the men don't know." He gestures down below. "The Spanish Treasure Fleet is here. I figure we sell our bounties to them, and we all get extra coin."

The Captain strokes his chin. The Treasure Fleet gets extra kickback for obtaining bounty, so selling them to the Fleet as opposed to the Crown is beneficial for both parties. *The Galleon Captains are terrible negotiators. They're around so much coin, they forget the value of a piece.* He pulls at the hairs of his beard. *But their extra coin won't buy the crew back for another voyage. There's plenty of money to be made at the gambling tables. They could very well make their money there and abandon ship.*

Carlos nudges him with his elbow. "What do you think?"

He shrugs. "Won't pay the crew's wages, I'll bet half of them will leave anyway." An idea strikes him. "Unless," he glances at Carlos. "How loyal are Moses and Henrique?"

He cocks his head to the side. "As loyal as they come, especially after the Englishman, why?"

Piranesi waves off his question. "Simple inquiry, just a simple inquiry." He returns to a pensive silence.

"I'll gather the crew then."

The men collect on the main deck in lines in front of Piranesi. Each with a new tall posture and puffed out chests. Moses especially stands with his chin held high.

Piranesi takes to his feet and leans heavily on his cane. The smell of the Spanish Treasure Fleet's crew assaults his nose in the sticky heat; and the stink of his own men overpowers his senses, making the stench nearly unbearable. He turns his face away from them all and takes a gulp of clean air before addressing them. *I'll address Danae's memorial first.* "You men all honored me with the memorial and sea burial of my wife and son. I cannot thank you enough for what all you've done."

The crew gives a solemn, single nod, and a moment of silence passes before Piranesi continues.

Their sorrowful expressions nearly pull a ribbon of guilt from his chest. But he puts it aside. "I want to allow you all some reprieve tonight. Go to shore, play cards and bring in as much coin as you can!"

This breaks the tension, and smiles break out amongst the men. A few begin to cheer.

Piranesi gives a small smile and bows his head. To allow them to get their own coin freely after a near mutiny is a risk. But necessary for the secondary part of his plan.

Moses and Henrique pass by so quickly, he nearly misses them.

"Moses, Henrique, wait!"

The boys turn around and approach.

"Aye Captain, is everything alright?" Moses shoves his hands in his pockets.

Piranesi gently shakes out his leg before responding. "You two are going to accompany Carlos to sell the bounties, to the Galleon Captains." He gestures at the first mate. "Once you do, you'll return here before joining the card games."

The pair glance at each other for a moment and Carlos walks up behind them.

"What's that Captain?"

Piranesi waves his hand. "Just telling them they're joining you to sell our bounties."

"Ah yes," he glances at the two younger boys and gives their shoulders a squeeze.

"Happy to do it, Captain!" Henrique pipes up.

"Absolutely." Moses agrees. "We will be back!"

Carlos grips the backs of their necks and steers them all towards the docks, and before long, they disappear from Piranesi's view.

He takes a seat on the quarterdeck and watches his men below. They blend in seamlessly with the Spanish sailors, and even the locals. *At least the Spanish born locals.* He remarks to himself. *There are a few natives among them that stand out like moscas en la leche.* He sniffs and wipes his nose. *I hear they're as pleasant as such.* He shrugs. No matter, it's a non-issue. His men will take them at dice or cards, and once phase two of his plan is complete, they'll be on their way.

He turns his gaze from the shore, the landsick that had plagued him since childhood still exists to this day. He swallows the bile, the panic, and quickly turns to the horizon to stop the seawater flooding his lungs. The rattling in his breathing stops. He takes slow, steadying breaths until the panic unravels.

He turns his chin towards the approaching sunset and allows his mind to wander to the weeks in and out of consciousness. *The dreams were so vivid.* All of them slightly different versions of the same thing. But the mirror at the end is what disturbed him the most. Mirrors are expensive, so he doesn't own one, but he's sure he doesn't look like that! He runs his tongue across his teeth. *All still there.* His hair is still full atop his head, and his skin most definitely has not melted off.
Still, the peculiar darkness of the dream itself, holds his attention.

He rests his chin back on his folded hands and tries to think to a time where the curse felt lighter. Andromeda's Daughter used to be a well-loved sight when he was young and alone, not a friend in the world and a father pre-occupied with the same visions he has now. Sightings of her were sparse at first. His freedom was well intact, or so he thought.
He wipes the accumulating sweat from his brow and

tries to ignore the obvious. She had overtaken his life; it was never really his to begin with.

Nothing was ever really yours, was it? Not your life, not your wife, not even your curse is truly yours. You just inherited the trouble.

The few of the crew below him catch sight of his intermittent glances and wave. He gives a halfhearted wave back before gazing back out to sea. Keeping the secret of his curse had been a vital part of his father's teachings growing up. *It's important*, he had said. *If anyone knew you can't touch land, they would take advantage of the weakness and you'd be killed.*

Piranesi snorts. Not too long after the curse had passed on, his father had tried to kill him to get the visions back. It could work, in theory. But he never fully got the chance. Carlos had stepped in.

He takes a shaky breath in, and scratches at his neck. Her absence is already starting to get to him. He's craving her like a drinker craves a bottle.

The sound of feet clomping back and forth as the sun sets pulls him from his thoughts.

A Galleon Captain stops in front of him and offers his hand.

"Pleasure doing business with you Captain Lumen, you never let us down."

He shakes the man's hand and gives a halfhearted grin. He's familiar with him, they frequently make deals that are mutually beneficial. "Always a pleasure Captain Iglesias." He nods. "You'll forgive me if I don't stand. Freshly crippled, you know." He smiles at his own lighthearted demeanor. "How's the family?"

The Captain glances back to shore. "Not a worry my friend, not a worry. As for the family, we are the only of the Iglesias clan that immigrated to the New World. Holds a high honor, knowing that anyone who carries the Iglesias name is one of mine." He crosses his arms proudly. "Quite the legacy if you ask me."

A flicker of jealousy ignites in his chest, but he shoves it away. "Not too much pressure?"

"Nah," he waves his hand and claps him on the back. "I have a good wife and amazing kids. They'll do right by me. How's your family?"

Piranesi avoids the man's gaze, hoping to sell his avoidance as grief. "They were killed by English Pirates." He slaps his thigh. "Same day I earned the bum leg."

"Ah." Captain Iglesias gazes down his nose at the leg in question. "That's a damn shame. I'm sorry to hear that. No monster quite like an Englishman."

"You have no idea."

An awkward silence permeates the air. A few moments pass without a word, and Captain Iglesias claps his back once more.
"Well, I must get going. I've a whole drove of silver from Potosi to deliver! The natives may be savages, and mostly barbaric to behold, but they're the most hardworking slaves we have yet."

He nudges Piranesi with an elbow. "Must be something in that blood of theirs that does them some good! Perhaps one day they'll work off their ancestral debts and earn a spot with the Lord like the rest of us."

He barks an order at his men to keep his new bounties in line before joining them ashore.

Piranesi watches him go. The simmering heat of envy rolls around in his gut and heats his cheeks. *Why does he get a legacy?*
He pictures the Iglesias family now: clean faces, wealth aplenty, a beautiful wife he chose for himself, that's entirely his own, and children who don't carry ancestral failures on their backs.

"Can we go play cards now, Captain?" Moses's voice interrupts his thoughts.

Ah yes, the second part of my plan. He clears his throat, the pitch would have to be perfect. "You boys have all grown close aboard my vessel haven't you?"

They exchange glances. "Yes?" Henrique responds.

Piranesi nods. "I thought so. You boys come with me." He beckons them forward, to the treasure hold. *It's a risk, and I have to take it.* The door squeaks open.

A small gasp escapes the boys. "They were right," Moses murmurs.

So they have been talking. "Who was right?"

Moses starts. "Nobody important, Captain. What does this have to do with us?"

Carlos meets them at the hold and crosses his arms. He raises his eyebrows expectantly. "Yes Captain, what is your plan?"

Piranesi closes the door. "Do you want this crew to stay together?"

The younger boys exchange a glance before responding. "Yes?"

"Then I need your help." He hobbles to the side of the ship and gesture to the shore. "What do you see?"

"People?" Moses offers.

"Ships too." Henrique adds.

"Exactly!" Piranesi claps him on the back. "Galleon ships to be exact. They carry silver, currency, from Potosi all the way back to Spain. They're loaded with coin!"

Moses's eyes grow wide. *Yes boy, yes. You're almost there.*

"You don't think they would notice just a few missing, right?"

Piranesi fights the smile that threatens to break on his face. "Can't imagine they would."

Carlos clears his throat. "And if we're caught?"

"We won't get caught!" Henrique crosses his arms. "We're stealthy."

"Yeah! We can do this!" Moses starts pulling at Henrique's arm. "We'll start at the tables! Get them good and drunk, take their money there, and sneak aboard!"

Henrique laughs. "You just want to get at the tables to see that merchant with the pretty wife!"

He shrugs. "He's a man with deep pockets, he sucks at Mentiras, and his wife is gorgeous. Now let's go!"

The boys race down the docks and towards the card tables, out of sight.

Carlos sighs and sticks his hands in his pockets. "I really hope you know what you're doing, Captain."

Piranesi hobbles back to the siderail to sit. "I didn't put the idea of stealing into their heads. They want to keep the family together. They're taking the risk on their own. You don't have to go."

"Of course I have to go!"

He ignores Carlos's tone and pulls a flask from his pocket. "Then be smart, swift, and don't get caught."

Chapter Six.

Piranesi watches the nightfall approach with his chin resting in his stacked fists. He fixes his eyes on the horizon, allowing his periphery to catch all movement. Henrique, Moses, and Carlos have been gone a few hours. Any moment he should be able to see them moving in the shadows, barely perceivable as they stalk the Spanish soldiers pacing back forth. He's been counting, as they should also be, as the soldiers make rounds around the Galleon.

He scratches his nose with his thumb. He catches sight of them as they slither up the ladder and haul themselves aboard into a covered lifeboat. A small flicker of hope sparks in his chest. *Perhaps if I can set off to sea, the visions will come back.* He rolls out his shoulders. He can't explain it, but the longer he goes without a vision, the more it feels like his blood is boiling in his body.

His men disappear over the side their movement ceases entirely. He relaxes for a moment. But getting aboard the Galleon undetected is only half the battle. If all goes well, they'll escape without a trace as well.

He allows his mind to wander, eyelids growing heavy. Perhaps, if he falls asleep, he can see her again. He knows he can hear her voice somewhere. She's calling his name now, he knows it...

"Captain!"

He jerks awake, his vision bleary. "What is it, Moses?"

"We need to go," he pants, his voice shaky. "Now!"

Without question, Piranesi leaps over the quarterdeck gate, resists the buckling in his leg, and barks commands belowdecks.

"Raise anchor and set us aloft!"

The Gods Curse comes to life as torches aboard the Spanish Galleon flicker.

He turns to Moses. "What happened!"

"Henrique was caught!" He shouts before sprinting away.

The blood drains from his face, leaving him cold. "Fuck!" His gaze turns back to the Galleon, the torches now converge to a focal point on deck as if surrounding something.

A scream pierces the air.

He skids to a halt, the light of the torches heats his face in waves before bathing him back in darkness. His heart pounds in his ears. *If I leave him the crew may turn on me, I'm dead without them.* More torches light the night. *If I stay, we're all dead.* He pulls at his hair. *This is an impossible fucking situation!*

"Captain!" Carlos and Moses sprint towards him. "What do we do!"

His straightens. "We have to leave him."

Moses stumbles and falls to his knees. "But Captain, he's my-"

"He knew the risks!" he interrupts. "If we go back now, we get the crew killed!"

Carlos balls his fists. "We're leaving half the crew if we go now anyway!"

Piranesi lunges, slamming his cane into the deck. "Who's the Captain here!"
Adrenaline courses through his body, humming in his blood.

Carlos shakes his head, and grabs Moses by the arm. "Who have you become?"
He drags the boy to his feet, shoving him to join the crew. He empties his pockets and tosses the sacks of silver at Piranesi's feet.
"Here's your coin. I hope it was worth it."

Carlos takes up the helm, and barks orders, directing their small cadre of men towards escape. The ship lurches forward and the wood groans against the sand.

"Open sails!"

Piranesi looks over his shoulder, the Galleon now fully awake. It too begins to lurch into action. He bites the inside of his cheek. *The Gods Curse is tied in speed to the Galleon at eight knots, if we let the Spanish catch up to us. Maneuverability is our only advantage.*

"Chase the sunrise, men!"

The ship lurches east and knocks Piranesi backwards. The wind snaps the sails at just the right moment to give them a head start. He pulls himself up with the help of the siderails, catching just the barest glimpse of some of the men he's leaving behind. Some of them chase the vessel, shouting and cursing his name. Others shrug and walk away. But it's the man who simply stares back at the ship as it chases the horizon that captures his attention. The lookout's silhouette stands still as a statue. Relief washes over him. *The only person who knows the truth is taken care of.* He blinks and the silhouette is gone. *Did he jump into the water?* He finishes standing up. That's ridiculous. He straightens, overlooking what's left of his crew.

They row east, sweat glistening on their young brows. *Once far enough out, we'll catch a westward wind and sail the opposite direction into the darkness.* He grips his cane and narrows his eyes, pushing down the sliver of guilt at leaving Henrique and the rest of the crew behind. *I sacrificed one man to save the many. I did what was best for the whole.*

The Galleon follows close behind. Piranesi tries not to get too comfortable. He can swear he feels the eyes of their crew on his back. One mistake could ruin them…

A sliver of light flashes in his periphery.

Her laugh claws at the outskirts of his mind.

No. Dread fills his stomach. *Not now.*

She leaps across the full line of his vision. Her thick black hair leaves an abyss of starless night behind her.

His heart pounds as the sound of their escape falls away to the wholeness of the vision:

She's always running.
He stretches out his fingers, flailing for her. The closest he's ever been to touching her.
He swears he can just grasp the loose coils of her hair.
His heartbeat thunders in his head, and he tries to shout for her. But as always, his voice is silent.
She laughs again and her image flickers up to the mizzenmast. His eyes follow her starlit trail. She stands on the crow's nest and ties a rope to her hips. She raises her arms like she's performing a grand show.
She jumps off. The intricate loops around her waist and legs hold her fast as she tumbles down gracefully to the deck, and lands without a thump. She throws her head back, and howls to the watching moon, and to someone else. Someone much smaller, but with the same dark hair. The same light in her soul.
He lunges.
But she's no longer there.

"No!" he screams and falls to his knees.

Carlos is at his side, grasping his arm and helps him to his feet. "What are you doing! Go to your quarters! The crew can't see you like this."

Piranesi knocks his head to the side. "No! Get back to your post! I'm fine!"

Carlos retakes the helm, his jaw tight and lips pursed. He makes a sharp turn of the wheel that nearly takes Piranesi off his feet.

"What the fuck do you think you're doing!" He charges his first mate. "Do I need to take the helm from you mate! It's me or the water!"

"We left them!" Carlos snaps in his face. "We left Henrique to die and abandoned the rest! How do you justify that, how do you sleep at night!"

Piranesi swings. Carlos's head snaps back. He shakes out his hand and stands over him. "Who is Captain aboard this ship!"

A loaded silence fills the air, and suddenly, Piranesi is very aware that he is being watched. The entirety of the crew stares in shocked silence. Most of them still have ropes in hand. Their eyes flit back and forth between the two men, waiting for one to submit.

Piranesi shifts his eyes to his downed friend. "You know I did this to keep the crew safe," he whispers. "If we stay here, we die. You know the Spanish won't let us live if they catch up to us."

Carlos rubs his jaw. "This isn't who you are, Nes. You're letting her get to you."
He rights himself and faces the crew. "You heard the Captain! Get back to work!"
The men hustle back to their posts, pointedly avoiding his gaze. He looks back at his Captain, the bruise already creating a knot on his jaw.
"I made a promise you know."

Piranesi unclenches his fists and allows his shoulders to drop just slightly. "Oh?"

Carlos dips his chin. "I promised Danae, before she left, that I'd keep you on the right path."

He raises his eyebrows. "You knew?"

Carlos furrows his brow, tears brim his eyes. "I delivered your son, Nes. I was there for them both when you couldn't be. Of course I knew. I just hoped you would tell me."

Piranesi turns away from him and takes a hobbling step towards the door. "Just keep us out of Spanish reach."

He locks the door behind him, before he sinks to the floor, and cries.

Chapter Seven.

The grey sky melts into a cloudy mist hovering over the azure water.

Piranesi leans on his cane, the handle digging into his side as he sits on the quarterdeck. The night had long passed in favor of what was supposed to be morning sunshine, though the sky remains grey. With the stars absent, and the sun cloaked with clouds, signs for north become a daydream. His mind fogs over as he replays the last argument he and Danae had.

"You're selfish, Piranesi! Everything you do, is only for yourself!"

"Everything I've done is to spare our son from this godforsaken curse! Isn't that why you tested

me in the first place!"

He rubs the burning sensation from his eyes.
It had been a frequent argument, seemingly on a loop
the last few months of their marriage. The constant
back and forth of his heart between his wife and his
love was exhausting, and it only got worse after
Vóreios was born.

He sits down on a barrel and hunches over; a
gargle in his stomach grows to a roar. He wills it to
pass. But his mind fills with color and shadow, of
dancing and tears, and he finds himself reaching for
what once was. He pounds a fist to his chest, trying to
make the ache stop as once again, his heart is pulled
in two directions.

*Oh Danae, you used to be able to make these
things go away.*
He snaps out of the thought, scolding himself for
wanting anything more than what he's destined.
The phantom-like visions persist in rapid succession
in response to his heart's betrayal. Too quick to catch,
yet too slow to ignore. Andromeda's Daughter, over
and over, and over again.

She had always been his only friend, even as his own father scoured the seas and used him as a compass, then eventually, tried to kill him when the curse passed on.

After his death, she was less of a friend, and more of a haunt. A persistent presence that he could always feel. He recalls the latest vision in the midst of his escape from the Galleon. The presence of the girl, presumably the daughter of his love, could only mean one thing: his curse is passing to the next generation, to Vóreios.

He coughs into his hands and tries to tamp down the jealousy. *The visions are strongest when we're young. We can feel everything we're supposed to be. All the love never received.*
He presses his palms into his temples, reminding himself of what's at stake if he continues. *This line of thought will only drive me mad. I won't be envious of my own son. I will not harm him like Atlas tried to harm me.*

His father's icy blue eyes had gone so wild, so crazed, that they hadn't even looked human anymore.

Piranesi shudders and forms a line in his mind. *No matter what happens, I will not harm my own son.* The gurgling in his stomach becomes quieter, and more manageable. He rests his head against the banister and surveys his crew. The way they get along like waves and wind, picking up where the other leaves off, not a care in the world for a millennium of curses on their backs. Minding only the next order to follow. *What would that be like?*

He turns towards the small bubble of laughter that floats from the helm to his ears. How does Carlos always seem to pull the best out of his men? Even with the thread of obedience he has left to pull from, Carlos can always manage to break the ice, ease the tension, and make the hardest of orders sound like a privilege to fulfill.

He rubs his hands together, trying to warm them with the friction. Andromeda's Daughter is always a constant push and pull between everything he ever wanted, and nothing he could live with. It made connecting difficult, even impossible. Especially if the wrong people found out that touching land would mean a death sentence for him.

Too easily would that be turned for another man's blackmail.

His mind flickers to memories of his wife, trying to find an ounce of comfort even in just her echoes. He rubs his temples, to this day he is still uncertain: Is she a pawn of the curse, or a stroke of redemption?

What even started that argument? What had I done wrong that time?

He huffs a breath, the cool air turning it into visible steam around his face. *There was never any making her happy. No matter what I did. She knew I was meant for another when she tempted me. And yet she still offered her hand.*

He pulls at his whiskers in irritation; a bald spot was beginning to form along his jaw. Even still, the sharp edges around his heart always soften for her. From the moment he saw her, standing on the water with a test and a wish, he had loved her. His cheeks warm.

She was all the magic I ever needed.

He turns his gaze to the water, allowing himself to get lost in the daydream. Her feet never sunk into the water, just stood atop it like the miracle she was. She was such a holy being, a Saint he never deserved.

His face runs cold. She had defeated every pining thought of Andromeda's Daughter. Every vision he had ever had, bowed down at her holy feet, and in an instant, he was ready to fall on his knees and worship at her temple. Yet she betrayed him in the end. She deafened his ears to his lover's cries, she blinded his eyes, she dulled his mind and diminished him to a simple man without a purpose.

She had twisted his stolen happiness and paid the debt he owes, to their son.
He spits over the ship's side. "Fucking Saint of the Sea, I should've taken the damn wish."
The Sea is always watching, and so am I.

"Captain!" a boy shouts from below, breaking him from his train of thought. "There's a ghost on the water!"

Piranesi snaps his attention to the sea. In the distance, a silhouette of a woman stands still as a statue. His heart kicks up a notch as he questions his own eyes. *Have I found her?*
He jolts to his feet, and a strike of lightning shoots up his leg. He winces, but hobbles forward.

"There, Captain!" the boy points. "Do you see her!"

He squints his eyes, and tries not to let his heart fall. The silhouette is too tall, the figure too thick. His shoulders slump. But a voice in his mind whispers, *if she's not here for you, who is she here for?*

Waves twist like the undertow in his stomach. *Saints of the Sea are only supposed to show up when sailors are going to be tested.*

A soprano song rings clear as a bell across the water, calling a man's name like a code word that only he will be able to understand.

Carlos steps off the quarterdeck and approaches the bow, each step as if in a trance.

Piranesi stands back, a sliver of that familiar feeling in his gut as the memory of his Saint's Test replays in his mind.

His first mate's eyes are already glassed over, and the world, he knows, consists of only the Saint in this moment. Carlos stretches his hand towards her.

She leaps from her place on the water, and steps onto the bowsprit, her form like a ribbon of light before appearing in front of them. Her gait is light as a feather, leaning slightly forward like a bird about to fly as she takes a few steps towards him. Her toes grip the wood as she balances atop it and accepts Carlos's outstretched hand.

She hops off the bowsprit and onto the deck, her feet don't make a sound.

The Saint gazes out at each crewmate, her eyes startlingly beautiful and illuminating. She fixes her stare on Piranesi.

For once, Andromeda's Daughter does not call, and for once, Piranesi does not wish her to.

When did Danae's deafening start to feel like drowning? It doesn't feel like that now.

A pang of longing lances his heart, but before he can focus on it for too long, the Saint speaks.

Her voice reverberates in holy resonance across the ship and crew. "Are you ready to be tested?"

Carlos straightens, the glassy look in his eyes sharpens. "I am."

The Saint turns to Piranesi and the crew, though he has the feeling her next words are weapons pointed in his direction. "You all may witness, but no one must interfere."

She pauses for a brief moment before she taps her bare foot to the deck.

The wind picks up. The water churns around them. A howl calls from the east.

The wood planks of the ship groan beneath his feet. The wistful feeling rips away for adrenaline to replace it. The God's Curse cracks beneath Piranesi's feet. He scrambles backwards.

Wood planks splinter down the center of the ship. He falls back on the quarterdeck steps.

The groaning intensifies, pulling his attention to the sails. *No god, please don't do this.*

The masts split.

Water fills the hull.

"No!" He staggers to his feet, to try to make the woman stop. A gust of wind pins him down, and forces him to watch.

Carlos stands, entranced and ignorant to the world, at the bow. He stares into the Saint's heavenly eyes for a moment more before she swipes her fingers across his eyes and breaks the spell.

His frame stiffens and he whips around, as if just noticing the state of the ship.

The sound of cracking wood fills the air. Piranesi has just enough time to grip the banister before The God's Curse snaps.

Piranesi clings to the ship, his feet dangle in the air as his men fall into the sea-filled hull. *What is she doing!*

He whips his head towards the woman in disbelief. Danae's tests for him were nothing like this, it was nothing... *Wait, what were my tests?* The memory fades like a vapor.

"Captain!" Carlos screams.

He's dangling with one hand gripping a plank. He kicks his legs as if he can fight the fall if he just rejects it hard enough.
A scream pierces the air as a young seaman slides past him.

Carlos releases the floorboard and goes after the boy. He stabs the dagger in his hand, into the planks at the same time he catches him. Piranesi can hear his shoulder *pop* from here.

Carlos howls into the air. "What are you doing!"

The Saint stands perched upon the bowsprit, which now sticks up out of the water at a sharp angle. "You have a choice to make, sailor." She sings.

Piranesi's stomach sinks. Danae's test is coming back to him now. *An impossible question,* and if Carlos answers wrong…

Her eyes flit to the opposite half of The Gods Curse. She locks eyes with the Captain.

No. Please.

"Save who matters most to you," she glances back down at Carlos, "or rescue those who you mean the most to."

The banister he's holding onto, cracks.

Time slows down.

Piranesi uses his cane to hook himself to another part of the railing.
"Save who matters most, or rescue those who you mean the most to."
What could that possibly mean!

But the memories come before he can stop them.
Carlos at his side, a steady hand on his shoulder as he lays his father to rest at sea. Carlos, enduring Danae's tests, and later officiating their wedding, pronouncing them. Carlos at his wife's bedside, delivering his son

while he watched through a bleary wall of visions. *He's always been there, he's always-*

Pain lances through his head at Andromeda's call.

Where were you? You stopped chasing me.

Chasing her? Piranesi shakes his head. *No that isn't right, that isn't right I never stopped, I never stopped!*

He freezes. He's right. He never stopped. Carlos delivered his son, *his* son! He took charge of the ship on so many occasions, the men look up to *him*, not Piranesi. *This was supposed to be mine! All of it! All of it was supposed to belong to me, and I have nothing!*

Come get me, I'm so close!

Please. He squeezes his eyes shut. *Shut up!*

"Please!" Carlos calls, breaking through the chaos. "I can't choose! I can't—"

Piranesi snaps his head up.

Can't choose? Can't choose!
Realization is a stone that shatters bones.

After all I've done, all I've sacrificed.
The feeling of Danae's soft hands at the altar, her finger fitting his mother's ring so perfectly. His son, purple-faced, tear-stained, and perfect, crying in his hands. *Did I ever get to enjoy it at all?*

He raises his chin to the wind.
There's nothing I didn't give up!
The corpses he defiled to cover their absence fill his nose with a rancid stench. His hands recall the beaded fat and sticky slip of blood.

Who have I been doing this for!
The Englishman he made take the fall, an innocent, bystanding life. Collateral damage. Useless. Pointless. It got him no closer. He still meant nothing to his crew.

Are you coming?
Her wretched voice rings in his ears and splits his head with lightning pain.

He kicks his leg into the side of ship. "Fuck!"
I've lost my family, I've lost my crew, not even my
first mate is on my side!
WHAT DO I HAVE LEFT!

His face warms as a gentle glow emanates
from the sea just a knot away from him.
Her face, finally in focus, as beautiful as he had ever
imagined it. She stands on a ship, tall and proud, a
man stands behind her with his arm around her waist,
and their daughter at her hip.
She's radiant, she's holy, she's—Carlos's words, from
before the English ship attacked, return to him.
Do you think she will love you, if she knows?

He stares into her celestial face, innocent of
everything he had done, clean from the sins he had
committed. The husband that stands proudly at her
back, and the daughter that looks up at them both
with equally pure eyes.
No. It strikes him. *She wouldn't. She already has*
everything. She has her place in the light.

He turns his face away and pulls a dagger
from his belt.

"I sacrificed everything for you." He growls. "Yet here you are, holy as the day you were born!"
He flips the knife in his hand.
"You have everything!" He howls at the clouds. "I won't be left with nothing!"

He throws his blade, and lets it fly true to its target.

The Saint drops to the floor.
Blood drips from her lips and onto the deck, the dagger protrudes from her neck.
The illusion breaks.

Piranesi crumples to the floor, no longer dangling. He glances out to sea, where he had seen Andromeda's Daughter. But she's no longer there. He struggles to regain his balance, and staggers to the bow.

Carlos rushes ahead of him to the Saint and cradles her head. "Who did this!" he cries, searching the crew for a guilty face. "WHO DID THIS!"

The men gather around, but no one comes forward. Piranesi remains stoic and silent. He glances down at her blank eyes and labored breathing. He shrugs. *What's one more, for a scrap of anything I have left?*

"Someone get the surgeon!" Carlos wails and pulls the blade from her neck. He presses his fingers over the spurting blood.

A young man rushes forward with a medical bag. Piranesi stops him with an arm.
"It's no use. She's gone."

"No!" Carlos cries. "Let him come, we can save her!"

Anger heats his chest and sets fire to his hands. *This is my ship. My home!*
He steps forward and kneels, making steely eye contact with his first mate. "I. Said. No." He rips Carlos's hand off the woman's neck.

"What are you doing Captain!" He wrenches his hand away and presses it back on the Saint's wound.

"That's an order!" Piranesi screams, nose to nose with his defiant first mate.

Carlos freezes in place and meets his Captain's eye. "No."

Disgust chokes the air from his lungs and escapes in a maniacal laugh. "No?"

The gun cracks before he realizes he's pulled the trigger.

Blood sprays out of the Saint's head. The crew stands in stunned silence.

"What have you done!" Carlos grabs fistfuls of grey mush and tries to shove it back into the gaping hole. "You killed her!"

Piranesi blows the smoke from the barrel and tosses the weapon to the floor. *And what about it?* He walks away, and says over his shoulder, "she was a threat to us all."

But Carlos stands with balled fists. "It was a test!"

"That you were failing!" Piranesi screams back.

The first mate backs away slowly. His bloodied hands drip to the crimson deck. "You were afraid I wasn't going to pick you."

The icy feeling of mutiny floods Piranesi's bones; at the same time the dark shadows of the crew and their traitorous spirits converge upon him.

He starts swinging.

A gust of swirling wind encompasses the ship, splitting the men apart before blood is shed.

Carlos gasps. "Where is she! She's gone!"

The mist clears and a fleet of Galleons surrounds them from all sides, each from less than a knot away.

"What's happening!" Moses screams.

"That damned Saint tricked us, boxed us in!" Piranesi swears.

The ships gain on them as each second passes.

"Open sails!" He commands his crew. "Half of you take to the hull and man the oars, Carlos take the helm!"

But all he gets, is silence, before each of them turns their gaze, to Carlos.

"Opens sails now!" Carlos takes over. "Let's get out of here, men!"

They scramble to follow his orders, but the wind is dead, the water is still, and the fleet approaches.

Chapter Eight.

"Stop! In the name of the Crown!"

Piranesi stands frozen in the face of a man, who, only a couple days ago he would have called a friend.

Captain Iglesias straightens his back. "We have come to take back what was stolen from the Crown."

Piranesi and Carlos share a glance, an ounce of camaraderie where moments before was only hostility. *His first mate's eyes seem to say, you got us in, only you can get us out.*

Piranesi steps forward and clears his throat. "Something was stolen, you say?"

"Yes, fifty pieces were taken from the treasury, and a man was caught." Captain Iglesias crosses his arms and leans forward, eyebrow raised. "Moments later your ship was seen leaving port."

"Hm," Piranesi scratches his chin, feigning confusion. "This is very disturbing news to me. I can't say I've seen your fifty pieces."

The men behind him stay silent, but he can feel their mutineering, bated breath, at his back. *Gnawing teeth waiting to strike.*

"That's very interesting," Captain Iglesias says, stroking his beard. He turns his back to The Gods Curse and whistles at someone behind him.

Henrique's face appears next to the Captain. Beaten and bruised, but unmistakable. Piranesi remains stone-faced, determined not to give anything away. The men hold their gasps behind him.

Captain Iglesias steers Henrique by the back of the neck. "This man says he knows nothing about your nighttime activities." He speaks to the boy in an animated, sarcastic tone.

"Can you believe that, boy? Is that right?"

Henrique stares straight ahead, not making eye contact with anyone. Captain Iglesias sneers and presses the barrel of a gun to his head. "Is that right, boy!"

Moses gasps as the rest of the crew draws their swords.

Piranesi grits his teeth and fights a yell. *Damn fools.*

The Galleon Captain smiles and withdraws the weapon. "Ah so you do know him then." He cocks his weapon and points it, staring Piranesi straight down the barrel.

"Tell me, bounty hunter, who is responsible? The Crown may not punish you for your cooperation."

Piranesi's mind is quiet. Is this another test? Another choice to make? The Saint is gone and Henrique stands alive before him, not dead. He searches his mind on how to react. But he feels nothing. The boy is merely a horn from the beast his crew had become. A thorn in his side, and a bastard wind steering him away from any kind of peace.

Moses sniffles behind him. *Saving Henrique means less than nothing.*
Piranesi picks his nails. At least if he starts from scratch his own life is intact.

"Well?" The Galleon's Captain prompts.

Piranesi raises his chin, and points at Carlos. "It was him, the traitorous swine!"

The crew holds their breath. The tension is thick as rope behind him, each gaze turns to the first mate.

Carlos stands locked in place, chest puffed out and chin held high. Piranesi can almost hear his self-righteous train of thought. Self-sacrifice is on his mind. He steps forward, prepared to take the fall.

"It was me!" Moses interjects and walks to the front of the crowd beating his chest. "I did it!"

"No, I did!" another boy shouts.

Piranesi fights a smile as, in satisfied silence, each predictable pawn sacrifices themselves for their king. *Yes. Remove yourselves from the board.*

Finally, Carlos he takes his turn, he steps forward. "It was me, sir."

The Spanish Captain looks down, meeting Piranesi's eye. Amusement etched plainly on his face. He shrugs.
"Have it your way then." He gestures at the other ships, loaded with firepower.

Dozens of firearms click into the ready position.
Captain Iglesias returns his gaze to Piranesi, eyebrows raised.
"You sure you had nothing to do with this, Captain?"

Traitors, every single one of them. Piranesi doesn't spare a second glance.
"My hands are clean of this."

Iglesias turns his stare to Carlos and juts his jaw in the direction of the quarterdeck.
"Go get the silver."

Carlos walks with his hands in the air to the treasure hold. He gathers the bags in his hands and carries it back to the opposing ship. He hurls them onto the Galleon, and resumes his place with his men, stone faced.

Captain Iglesias raises a brow and surveys his fleet. "Spare the Captain," he shouts. "Shoot the rest."

Pop after pop, snaps in Piranesi's ears, ringing like cathedral bells banishing him from confession.

He would not speak either way.

Gunsmoke fills the air and the sweet smell of charcoal twisting around the rot of sulfur permeates his senses as gun powder rains down.
He does not watch.

Thump after thump hits the deck in a wet sticky heap, until Henrique is all that stands.
He stares straight into his eyes.

Iglesias cocks the hammer.
The final pop is punctuated by the side of Henrique's head.

Blood and grey mush slops down the side of the Galleon and collects in the water.

Drip.   *Drip.*   *Plunk.*

Piranesi stares unblinking. Everything is ringing. Everything is quiet.

Boots thud on deck in front of him as Iglesias approaches. Blood squelches beneath his feet at every step. His gaze remains forward.

"You're lucky you're worth more to the Crown alive." Iglesias whispers in his ear, his eyes flicking up and down his frame.
"You didn't fool me, Captain."

Piranesi shifts his eyes to meet his but says nothing.

The Captain beckons his men forward. One with a leather bag of burning coals, and the other with a heated brand.

Iglesias takes the brand from his officer's hand and swings it slightly in the air.
"You know, we usually only use these for slaves." He

sinks the metal brand into the bag of coal.
"But I'll make an exception."

He juts his chin to the same officer he took the
brand from, and he grabs Piranesi's right arm, baring
his wrist.

Piranesi doesn't struggle, her merely stares off
in a resigned disinterest.

Iglesias pulls the brand, red hot from the bag.
"Hold still."

Searing pain registers somewhere in Piranesi's
mind, but he does not move. Does not yell, but stays
stone-faced and still.

When Iglesias pulls the brand away, Piranesi
spares a glance. Red hot blisters in the shape of a
patriarchal cross now brand his wrist.

Captain Iglesias levels a cool stare at his
captive. "I hope this," he taps the blisters and sends a
jolt of pain up Piranesi's arm, "serves as a reminder
of who you work for."

He turns to and tosses a bag of silver at his feet.

"Take this as an advance of payment," He calls over his shoulder, "for your next bounty—and buy yourself a better crew. One with less..." he rolls his eyes, considering the word to use, "thieves."

Chapter Nine.

"I had really hoped I was wrong."

Danae's disembodied voice sends a chill down his spine.

"Where are you!" Desperation rips through his throat and leaves a bitter taste on his tongue. He paces back and forth; his boots stick to the deck with every bloody step.

"I said where are you!"

She sits perched on the bowsprit, her long hair the color of caramel candy, and her eyes as sharp and green as his coveted earth. She draws her shawl tighter around her shoulders.

"Even after everything, I still had hope you would make the right choice."

He glances back and forth between the bodies and his wife.
"What are you doing here? How did you find me?"

She hops off the bowsprit, her bare feet avoiding pools of blood and flesh. She lifts her skirt to keep the crimson from the white cloth. She stands a foot away from him, peering up at his face, unrecognizable from the man she married.
"Do you not remember what I said? I gave you a warning."

Be careful the nets you cast, Piranesi.
He turns away from her. "I don't know what you're talking about."

"Yes, you do." She closes the gap between them. "I told you I was watching."

The Sea is always watching, and so am I.
His pulse races in his veins. He releases a nervous chuckle. "So, you had one of your Saint friends come and test my men, set me up to lose it all and when I

do what I have to do, you show up to shame me. Typical."

She puts her hand on his shoulder, and his blood runs ice cold, the new brand on his wrist the only source of heat left in his body.
"What friend?"

He whips around to see the Saint he shot in Danae's place. He blinks and a young man stands before him.

He staggers back. "The lookout."

She drops the illusion, but the lookout's voice comes from her lips.
"I all but told you my test was starting when I hinted at a code word."

He pants, sweat drips from his temples and runs down his cheeks. "But you left. You couldn't have been the lookout, you and Vóreios were both gone! He stayed on the ship until Acapulco!"

Danae cocks her head. "Did he? After that night, did you see me again?"

Piranesi wracks his brain, trying to poke holes in her story. Had he seen the lookout? He could have sworn he saw him in the hull, over breakfast, at a table, murmuring among the men. Anything!

But his mind remains blank, and the pieces all fall into place. He advances toward her.
"You said Saints give a series of three tests! You left the ship; how can you possibly test me when you're not here to see the results."

Danae stands her ground, but answers in a whisper. "The stars see everything, and the water never forgets."

Phantoms rise from the water. The slaves. The Englishmen. His crew. Carlos.
They appear in vapors of blood and sea, replaying his actions. The bodies, the Galleon, the Saint's test. The death of his crew.

"You had three tests!"

The Englishman stands before him, covered in the bodies he shredded as he tries to scream his innocence. He watches himself attack to cover up his lie.

"Three impossible questions Piranesi!"

The empty treasure hold lays barren moments before he abandons half his crew. All to save his own skin from a scheme he planted in the mind of a young boy.

"You failed them all!"

Andromeda's Daughter passes by, so painstakingly close. He cold have called for her, could have gotten her attention and the curse would have all been over.
But he turns the knife in his hand, and gunfire follows with the bodies of his men making up the echoes of each round.

He falls to his knees and looks up at his wife. "I didn't know. That's not fair, I didn't know!"

Danae brushes a tear away from his cheek with her thumb. "Dearest, that was the point."
She turns to go, disappear into the sea once more.

He stands. "Don't walk away from me! This means nothing! It's you screwing me over once again!"

"Excuse me?" She laughs. "I gave you everything you asked for that night!"

The memory encapsulates them in a vortex. Piranesi is swept away by the winds and the way they carry her voice.

"You've changed! You would never pass any tests you were given now, you wouldn't be worthy of consideration!"

"Everything I've done is to spare our son!"

She whips around on him, her long braid swings like a rope. "Everything you've done is to serve yourself!"

He balls his fists. "You just want to hold me back! Deafen the curse like you've always done! This is all by your hand!"

She laughs coldly. "You want me gone? You want to cut your anchor loose and get swept away?

Don't test me, I will leave."

He leans in. "Do it. Leave me to my devices and my victory will be attained. You think you're my anchor, but all you do is hold me back."

She meets his eyes. "Be careful the nets you cast, Piranesi. The Sea is always watching, and so am I."

The vision melts away. The Gods Curse returns, stagnant and bloody on a windless sea. He turns on his heel, searching in every direction for his wife.
"Danae?"

But she doesn't answer.
A wind picks up from the east with a whisper that dances in his ears. Piranesi looks at his bloodstained hands, and the brand blistering his skin. The call that had plagued his heart sits in a cold silence.

The bodies cool and blood pools in the center of the ship towards his feet.
Finally, the fog clears completely and reality sinks into his skin.

He is well, and truly, alone.

Acknowledgements.

Firstly, I need to thank to the stars and back, my wonderful, awesome, kickass of an artist sister, Trinity for being the best cheerleader, alpha reader, and best friend I could ask for. You hurt my feelings, a lot, but I couldn't have done this without your encouragement, your reading and re-reading of each iteration of this story, and of course, our brainstorming sessions while Criminal Minds played in the background. Also, the cover you made for this story

Secondly, my beta readers, Anna, and Jordan, your guys' feedback was so encouraging, so amazing, I can't thank you enough for taking the time to sit and read my work. I love you guys, and I'm so honored to be a friend and writing comrade.

Now, my demolition's expert and writing coach, Tim. *deep heavy sigh* You hurt my feelings. However, your feedback helped shape what this story is now. It would not be as good without your help, so I appreciate you, your tutelage is worth at least ten camels. (double humped).

Last but certainly not least, I would like to thank my wonderful husband, for whom our favorite character is named: Carlos.

You pushed me to continue, you supported my drive, and you listened intently as I read the manuscript out loud. You put up with all the late nights with my face illuminated by a screen, lost in a world you couldn't join me in yet, and welcomed me back from my long voyages with open arms. Te quiero mucho, mi lindo Tesoro.